Edith Matilda Thomas

A Winter Swallow

With Other Verse

Edith Matilda Thomas

A Winter Swallow
With Other Verse

ISBN/EAN: 9783743441866

Manufactured in Europe, USA, Canada, Australia, Japa

Cover: Foto ©Andreas Hilbeck / pixelio.de

Manufactured and distributed by brebook publishing software
(www.brebook.com)

Edith Matilda Thomas

A Winter Swallow

A WINTER SWALLOW

WITH OTHER VERSE

A WINTER SWALLOW

WITH OTHER VERSE

BY

EDITH M. THOMAS

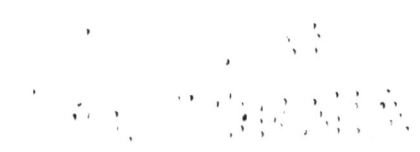

NEW YORK

CHARLES SCRIBNER'S SONS

1896

CONTENTS

v

CONTENTS

CONTENTS

A WINTER SWALLOW

" How much do I admire the generous humor of Chelonis, daughter
and wife to Kings of Sparta! Whilst her husband, Cleombrotus, in the commotion of her city, had the advantage over
Leonidas, her father, she, like a good daughter, stuck close to
her father in all his misery and exile, in opposition to the con-
queror. But as soon as the chance of war turned, she changed
her will with the change of fortune, and generously turned to
her husband's side ; whom she accompanied throughout ; having, as it appeared, no other wish than to cleave to that side
that stood most in need of her, and where she could best man-
ifest her compassion.

—MONTAIGNE *On Experience.*

CHARACTERS

LEONIDAS . . .	King of Sparta.
CLEOMBROTUS . .	Son-in-law of Leonidas, and usurper of the throne of Sparta.
CHELONIS . . .	Daughter of Leonidas, and wife of Cleombrotus.
ÆGLE and CLEON . .	Children of Cleombrotus and Chelonis.
PRIEST OF POSEIDON.	

Various Voices of the People.

SCENE

The Temple of Poseidon where CLEOMBROTUS, *on the restoration of* LEONIDAS, *has taken refuge. The walls are hung with pictured memorials of ship-wreck and rescue, offered by those who have escaped the dangers of the sea. From time to time hymns and ascriptions to the God are heard, issuing from the depths of the temple.*

A WINTER SWALLOW

CLEOMBROTUS.

Vain is their hope, who seek, in modern days,

To breathe into the current civic life

The glorious spirit of an ancient State,

Single in faith, in honor absolute,

And shining with the pristine light that draws

From out the Golden Age.   What shall avail,

When evil grow the customs, and the laws

Wax supple in the hands that fear them not!

Ah, Agis, thou my leader in Vain Hope!

Brave was the thought and generous the design,

To win for Spartans their prime heritage,

Equality in wealth, and place, and power.

3

But all has come to naught, thro' trust betrayed—

The people and ourselves alike betrayed,

Leonidas restored, and thou and I

Brief sanctuary craving from the Gods;

Thou, underneath Athena's brazen roof

(Like to the heaven that frowns upon thy cause)

I, in Poseidon's temple; while each one,

Bereft of other, Vengeance close pursues.

[*Here a voice is heard in the inner temple, chanting delivery from the sea.*]

Lord of the limitless waters,

   I was sinking down to my grave,

When one of thy gentler daughters

   Reached out her hand, to save!

God of the savage surges,

   That beat up the azure plain,

With a wind behind them that urges—

   A goad, and the shaken rein!

4

In their rage they were trampling me under,

    When Ino arose on their path—

And their phalanx was broken asunder,

    And they were thrown back in their wrath.

Then on a billow uplifted—

    Smooth as the flight of a dream,

As the sea-weed the tide has drifted

    Up the still course of a stream,

The silvery arms of a river

    Received me, and laid me to sleep

Where the reeds in the sunlight quiver

    And faint comes the moan of the deep.

[CHELONIS *has entered, and now slowly glides across the foreground of a painting representing the rescue of Ulysses.*]

CLEOMBROTUS.

    What moves across yon pictured curtain, where

    The struggling mariner lifts his prayer for aid?

    Chelonis?—Nay ; some cloud upon the brain

5

But shapes her rising, like Ulysses' hope,

From the white anger of the wind-lashed sea,

To yield the talisman that smooths his way.

Oh, wrecked am I, whose senses chaos shakes;

For still my sight the breathing image feigns

Of sweet Chelonis, with her eyes in tears,

And flower-like hand in pity reached toward me.

I'm overwrought.   I will look otherwhere,

Lest melancholy fancy madness grow.

I'll think this hour she sits among her maids,

Restored, and Sparta rings with her just praise.

I'll think (for ne'er so warm and quick a heart

To fame attunes its pulses as to love)—

I'll think how at her feet our children play.

Some little grief the lisping one repeats,

And on his fair soft locks her kisses fall.

Oh, lost to me—oh, more than kingdom lost !

[CHELONIS *makes a slight movement forward, and speaks in a low voice.*]

Nay, found to thee, because of kingdom lost !

CLEOMBROTUS (*still with face averted*).

    Did she not speak? But I will not look up.

    The worst befalls when sovereignty of self

    Retires, and darkness surges thro' the brain :

    Yet, so, the hounds of stern Leonidas

    A madman, and not me, should bring to bay.

CHELONIS (*approaching, touches the arm of* CLEOMBROTUS).

    Cleombrotus, no longer doubt what is ;

    For I am here, this hand my hand, and these

    The lips that thou, and no man else, shall greet.

CLEOMBROTUS.

Why shouldst thou come, my soul? What draws thee

    here ?

CHELONIS.

    Grief, grief and love for thee—thy need, my love !

    Has drawn me here. I rested not when once

    I saw thee naked to the hissing lash

    Fate flings at random round our Spartan world,

    Where just and unjust feel, by turns, its smart.

Or just, or unjust, how can I divide?

A woman, I, alas, but know my house,

Divided, falls, and hearts are crushed beneath.

I saw thee, as I did my father see,

That night I glided from thee in thy sleep,

Nor, lightly kissing, woke thee to oppose;

But made all haste to reach my father's side,

—An exile, whose embittered idle lot

My utmost service might a little soothe;

But I in far Arcadia pined for thee.

CLEOMBROTUS.

Oh, freely didst thou leave me in the hour

Of hope supreme, of triumph, when thy name

With mine should have commingled on Fame's lip!

And com'st thou freely now, when I am naught?

CHELONIS.

Ah, then, thou wast not mine so much as now.

Thou hadst for wife the daughter of Pride and Power,

—Glory hadst thou for wife—I, but the child

Of that Leonidas, deposed, contemned,

So thou and Agis might break better days

For Sparta (have they dawned, alas !) ; but he

Ascendant now, no more hath need of me.

And I have come to thee—to share what fate is thine.

CLEOMBROTUS.

 Chelonis, thou art truant but to joy ;

 To grief thou dost desert, as others wont

 To fly where all delight hath beckoned forth.

 Thou art a swallow whom the shortening day

 And the bleak North allure ; with dauntless breast

 And single thought, beating against the storm ;

 While all thy fellows seek the summer South.

 My Winter Swallow, where's the nest for thee ?

CHELONIS.

 Even amid the ruin where thou art,

 I build my home and sing against the storm.

 I'm glad my father is called back again ;

 And nothing shall I fear, to bide with thee,

Though, haughty in return of power, his hand

Rest heavy on us both.—Cleombrotus,

Be sure, the storm will break.

CLEOMBROTUS.

                    I heed the storm,

But more I heed thee singing in the storm.

Now, would to Phœbus and the Sisters Nine,

I bore the gift of song within my breast !

Then should Chelonis with Alcestis stand,

With Iphigenia and Andromache.

Thy name should darken hers by Homer sung—

That Helen, whom our Sparta bred, and Troy

A baleful light in Ilion's watch-tower set.

All men that in the coming time should read

Old annals of the wondrous loves of old,

Should turn from hers away, to dwell on thine,

And make thy very memory blush with praise !

CHELONIS.

Cleombrotus, men still would more praise Helen.

That knowest thou, or else, less man thou wert !

10

All men praise Helen, till their doom she sounds,

And even then to some she stands exalt

As Venus Victrix, conquering all who live.

None but some woman, in the after-time,

Who loves as I do—scourged for love indeed,

Yet full content—shall give one thought to me.

Ah, poor Chelonis, matched with her of Troy !

Hereafter, if the Gods shall ever grant

A light hour and a merry heart once more,

My love, I'll change a jest with thee, on this.

CLEOMBROTUS.

My ear deceives me, or a child's voice starts

Through the long murmur of Poseidon's house.

[*The children enter.*]

ÆGLE.

Mother, I pray you, stay no longer here ;

The voices and the echoes frighten me.

My little brother wakes, and sobs, and sobs ;

I've said, " Hush, hush," and " Sweetheart, do not

cry "—

11

Just as you always say, to quiet him—

And given him shells to play with—corals too,

And those white bones of fishes, quaint in shape,

The children of the Sea for playthings have.

But still he weeps.   O mother, take us home.

CHELONIS.

Dear child, bring little Cleon here to me.

Most wisely, sweetly, have you played the nurse.

Now, kiss your father's hand, and lay your own in his.

CLEOMBROTUS (*embracing the little girl*).

Darker, my little Ægle, are those locks

Than when, unknowing, I caressed them last.

A year has barely passed.   In some few days

Thy father's temples the reverse shall show.

(*To the little boy.*)

Come hither, little man, what canst thou do,

Thy blue eyes shining brave thro' all thy tears?

CLEON.

I can play the lute, and walk around the world !

ÆGLE.

> Father, he cannot ! When he plucks the strings,
>
> They make an angry buzzing ; and he thinks
>
> Our garden-ground at Tegea is the world !

CLEON.

> And where my father goes, I will go, too !

CLEOMBROTUS.

> I wake, I come unto myself, at last !
>
> What do they here—these lambs ; and what dost thou,
>
> Chelonis ! surely, in thy hurried flight,
>
> Upgathering them with fond, distracted heart,
>
> Thou didst not use thy gift of presage keen.
>
> One doom apace shall draw them down with us,
>
> More surely than if now we were afloat
>
> On rudest raft, in the gray God's demesne.

CHELONIS (*seating herself at the feet of* CLEOMBROTUS).

> Cleombrotus, abide the event, then judge
>
> If I have erred, or lost in presage keen.

The children have their part to play in this,

Nor are less moving in their dear effects

For knowing not they have a part to play.

Sit here, my little Ægle, on this side;

My little, teasing, roguish Cleon, here.

(*To* CLEOMBROTUS.)

If e'er thou trusted, now put forth thy trust;

I hear the soldiers in the outer court.

(*A Brief Interval.*)

[*Enter* KING LEONIDAS, SOLDIERS, PRIESTS, CITIZENS—
an excited and vehement throng.]

A VOICE.

Strike down the wretch, wherever he may lurk;

Spare not.   He spared not to thrust out our King,

The loved Leonidas.

ANOTHER VOICE.

Less said were best,

My valiant Sir; for there be present here,

14

Who can remember how thy voice acclaimed,

" Cleombrotus," and still, " Cleombrotus!

Behold the just Lycurgus come again ! "

A PRIEST OF POSEIDON'S TEMPLE.

Give ear to mercy, King Leonidas,

Soon past are all men's days beneath the sun.

Haste not a mortal's never-staying feet.

This is the precinct of the God.   Beware,

Lest never should thy hands be clean again,

If once ensanguined in a holy place.

A VOICE.

Heed not the priest, O King ; thy vengeance take.

Poseidon sways the waters, not the earth.

ANOTHER VOICE.

But he can shake the earth, thou impious one,

And he hath terrified both Gods and men.

A SPECTATOR.

What is that drooping shape in sable robe,

Unsearchable to me as veilèd Fate ?

ANOTHER SPECTATOR.

Those be the children of Cleombrotus,

I'd say, who cling unto that drooping shape,

But that I know they with their grandsire dwell,

They and their mother, safe beneath his roof,

And far away from such heart-straining scenes.

FIRST SPECTATOR.

Hush, see, some sudden passion shakes the King !

LEONIDAS.

Thou canst not be my daughter !   What ! thou art ?

And here ?   My daughter, art thou traitor turned ?

CHELONIS (*rising and casting her veil aside*).

Oh, no !   The daughter of Leonidas,

Until that name he rases from his heart,

And even then, in mine it greenly dwells.

LEONIDAS.

Leave, then, that recreant, and return to me !

CHELONIS.

Daughter am I ; but wife, a dearer name,

I also bear since ever from that day

When thou didst give me, from thy blessing hand,

To this Cleombrotus thy wrath pursues.

LEONIDAS (*turning to* CLEOMBROTUS).

Say not my wrath alone.   Great Nemesis

That hath the hound's scent for the traitor's track,

And fleetness of the hound, and naked fang,

Cleombrotus, pursues thee for thy crime.

Gave I not all thou hadst, in giving thee

Honor, and power, and deference to thy voice,

Both by the people and thy peers observed ?

What word of thine, or Agis', for thy King

Was spoken, when the *ephori* returned

From that grave session 'neath the silent stars

They hold each ninth year, on a moonless night ?

Ay, when Lysander, of the crafty soul,

With grievèd looks, in broken words, announced

17

The stars themselves had shot an argent shaft,

Which portent, none might doubt, condemned the King,

Saidst thou, " The lore of Heaven hath other seers,

Who read, ' That shaft, belike, was meant for thee ! ' "

Nay, but the silver ring of thine apt speech

Even then, was heard to promise debts forgiven,

Lands redistributed, and rank erased ;

Alien and native-born, patrician, slave,

The arts that sing and shine, and lumpish toil—

Yea, best and worst—merged in one level drear.

" Lycurgus " was thy watchword, and thy sword

" Lycurgus "— now " Lycurgus " be thy shield !

Among the shades he blushes to behold

Himself to earth returned in such as thou !

What to thy King and father dost thou say,

Ere steel shall send thee to Great Minos' seat ?

[*A pause, in which* CLEOMBROTUS *remains silent, not so much as lifting his head.*]

He speaks not, nor will speak.   Soldiers, advance.

CHELONIS.

    I to my King and father—I would speak ;

    For him whose guilt be also on my head,

    For these who guilt have never known, would speak.

                       (Indicates the children.)

SPECTATOR.

    My eyes are full.   The sight of her brings tears ;

    But she has none herself.   Old gossips say

    Such dearth bodes ill.   I would that she might weep.

PRIEST.

    Much hath she suffered—restless grief her lot,

    Who, loving both, is flung by adverse fate

    Between two warring ones.   Relent, and hear.

                       (To the King.)

LEONIDAS.

    Estranged art thou by thine own froward choice,

    No more my daughter ; yet, because thou hast

    Her voice and tender likeness, do thou speak.

19

CHELONIS.

My lord, the King, dost thou this raiment know?

It is the sable dress wherein I walked,

Or sat, and wept with thee, or sadly smiled,

When we abode in Tegea.   Thou didst wish

The rose that bloomed against the garden-wall,

Might lay her crimson by, and put on black,

To sort with thee and thy most mournful state.

Roses were on my cheeks, light in these eyes,

Ere that thy wrongs and sorrows chid them hence.

Think'st thou that for Cleombrotus I chose

This raiment, and have worn it ever since?

Thou knowest for whose sake I put it on.

Sorrow and wrong from thee are fallen away,

And thou art King of Sparta, as of old.

But dost thou think these sables I can change

For boon attire, and bind my locks with gold,

And look on triumph and high festival,

While, sent by steel to Rhadamanthus' seat,

I mourn for him thy hand did give, and take,

Whom first I loved, and last, with such increase

As bounteous Summer, heaping store on store,

Sets in compare with promissory Spring.

A SPECTATOR.

Where is the heart in King Leonidas?

Mine molten is within me, at these words.

ANOTHER.

Hush! Kings are not as we are, thou shouldst know.

All hairy was the heart of him of old—

That brave Leonidas who held the Pass.

But listen to the Princess; still she speaks.

CHELONIS.

And never, never, shall that hour befall

When I shall mourn for lost Cleombrotus;

Since, if his true repentance, sacred oath,

And bonded fealty avail not, nor

These deep-drawn sighs for pardon, on my lips,

Nor the mute pleading of these little ones,

Then shall Cleombrotus himself endure

More grievous punishment than thou canst serve,

For I before his eyes will let life forth,

And enter first the precincts of the night !

I will not suffer it that maids and wives

Of Sparta shall salute me with these words :

" We pity thee, unfortunate Chelonis,

Large virtues for thy dower, yet poor, we trow,

In sweet persuasions such as we could wield ;

Since both thy husband and thy father stood

Unmoved, and threw contempt on all thy prayers.

Wretched art thou, as daughter and as wife ;

We in thy place had pleaded not in vain."

So would they speak, if I would live to hear.

My King and father, do the Gods entail

Madness with wearing of a diadem,

So that the glittering circlet is more worth

Than life and weal of those once dear to thee?

If this be true, 'twas the same frenzy moved

Cleombrotus, when envious hands he laid

Upon that fatal badge of sovereignty.

I can no more.   My voice is less than theirs,

Who in this temple void of joy entreat

The eldest of the Gods, hedged round with dread,

And most remote, to prayers of earthly men.

[*She takes her seat on the ground beside* CLEOMBROTUS.
*There is an interval in which is heard the chanted
prayer of one who has a ship at sea.*]

Saturnian tamer of the chafing tides,

That wear away the land upon all sides !

They rise, they fall, or at thy bidding stand—

Oh, what to thee, that, in thy rugged hand,

Thou holdest more than all the countless prize

That in thy never-rifled coffer lies ?

How bitter is thy heart, how cold thy lip,

            Yet, oh, preserve my ship !

For not with gold, nor with long-ripened wine,

Rich-laden, I that ship to thee consign.

23

Oh, more than life—my love she bears afar !

Raise not the mists nor hide the pilot-star;

Nor let the whirlpool's fatal eddy draw,

Nor rock impale ; nor send the sudden flaw.

How bitter is thy heart, how cold thy lip,

Yet, oh, preserve my ship !

But if to Ægas, where thy palace bright

Fills the blind nether sea with golden light,

Thou bear my love, and charm to endless sleep,

Soon will I follow, down the breathless deep,

And be forever where my love abides.

Saturnian tamer of the foaming tides,

How bitter is thy heart, how cold thy lip,

Yet, oh, preserve my ship !

SPECTATOR.

See how the Princess lays her cheek 'gainst his,

For whom she has both dared and borne so much.

Ye Gods ! blest is Cleombrotus, indeed,

Though life be stricken from his grasp this hour.

ANOTHER.

> So have I seen, when in the chase embayed,
>
> Some hapless creature, bred in greenwood aisles,
>
> Fall in the open, while the dart flies home.
>
> One look upon her slayers round she casts,
>
> Ere the bright guileless eye in darkness shuts.

LEONIDAS (*after consulting aside with his friends pro-
nounces sentence upon* CLEOMBROTUS).

> Henceforth thou art an exile and an alien,
>
> To whom no more the sight of Sparta's hill,
>
> With the great temple crowned and glorious ;
>
> Nor the long valley with the plane-tree clothed ;
>
> Nor wreathèd smoke from Sparta's hearths upborne !
>
> Be grateful thou, who might'st from life have been
>
> An exile fleeing in the leaden boat
>
> Which no returning pilgrim e'er hath borne.
>
> Thou owest this of Clemency to her,
>
> Whose bruisèd soul hath known too much of grief :
>
> Take back thy life, that else had forfeit been.

Now, my Chelonis, come away, come, come!

Thou hast the boon of breath for him obtained,

And luminous art thou with mercy's light.

Be joined no more unto that wretched man.

Thy father's roof and years of blessed peace

Henceforth for thee and for thy little ones.

Uprise, and come, my daughter.

CHELONIS.

No, no, no !

The boon thou gav'st is not to him alone.

Where'er he breathes the air, I breathe the same,

And the lone path shall double footprints show.

And these, my children, 'neath their father's roof,

Though 'twere some bleak unsheltered Thracian hut,

Shall pass their youth, as I with thee passed mine,

And say whene'er they will, " My father's house ! "

CLEOMBROTUS.

Let me go forth alone.   It is not meet

That two should suffer, when but one is doomed.

CHELONIS.

There is but one, when thou and I go forth.

LEONIDAS.

Hear me! I, by thy mother's sacred name,

Conjure thee, pass not from my sight away.

Thy mother's memory points thy course to thee.

CHELONIS.

That memory hastes me on in my resolve.

. When failed she ever from her husband's side?

(*To the King.*)

Farewell—oh, father—yet farewell, farewell.

I see, I know, there is no way but one.

(LEONIDAS *and attendants retire, and the guards sur-round the little group which remains behind.*)

Cleombrotus, thou hast thy punishment

Upon that head which late usurped a crown;

But take therewith what comfort comes with me.

There may be light beyond the gloomy verge

Of all we see of heaven.

CLEOMBROTUS.

Thou Star of Sparta,

Night, with thee beaming, far outshines the day !

Yet, Oh, that thou shouldst sink adown the sky,

To be my lamp alone, in obscure ways !

Remain.   Live thou renowned in Lacedæmon !

CHELONIS.

In vain thou urgest (save thou bear me hate).

Aught else is past my will that I should do.

Chelonis goes not, neither stays : it is

The woman in Chelonis sets her fate :

That arbiter decides—and we go forth.

THE CHILD ÆGLE.

Do we go with my father, where he goes ?

I can walk far, and never stop to rest.

One day I walked from where Fear has her altar

To Laughter's little sunshine temple, where

The water-clock sings like the sweetest birds,

And every kind of bird comes to be fed.

'Tis a long distance, yet I was not tired.

CHELONIS.

'Tis longer where we go, my little Ægle,

But look! your father's arms are waiting for you.

My baby-boy well knows his nestling-place.

Lead forth, O Guards, where'er the King commands.

Yet stay a moment.   It is fit, methinks,

That we, Cleombrotus, before we go

(Though gifts are none, in hands so bare as ours),

Should pay our homage to the gray Sea God,

Whose threshold is the last that we shall cross

In Lacedæmon.   Thence, what God shall lead?

LYRICS

THE ROSES OF PIERIA

"But thou shalt ever lie dead, nor shall there be remembrance of
thee, then or thereafter ; for thou hast not of the roses of Pieria."
—*From The Bibelot, compiled by Thomas B. Mosher.*

THUS Sappho wrote to maid, or dame,

Of Mitylene, well forgot :

" When dead, thou shalt be dead to fame,

So, dead, indeed ; for thou hadst not

The Roses of Pieria."

Who was she, dame or maid, for whom,

A few sweet mortal flowers resigned

Their sunlit day, to deck her tomb ;

For whose calm brows were never twined

The Roses of Pieria ?

33

Thou subtle Lesbian ! happier far

   Was she than thou, whom yet men sing,

Leucadia's misty, mournful star

   Whose hand did gather, by the spring,

     The Roses of Pieria.

Why spak'st thou not the word that warns,

   Ere woman takes the Muses' pledge ?

Why saidst thou not, " There are no thorns,

   Thou hapless one ! like those that hedge

     The Roses of Pieria ! "

A BIRTHDAY HEALTH

OH, never the glass with the falling sands,

   To measure the heart-warm hour for thee ;

But the beaded wine in the light, as it stands,

   Crowned with the rose, thy horologe be.

For the bubbles arise, as the moment takes wing,

   And they seem to say, in their crystalline art,

" Three things in the world are ascendant : a spring,

   The bubble of wine—and youth in thy heart ! "

A HOME-THRUST

"BE constant, constant," in the spring he urged ;
And when the season in full summer merged ;
And when the dry leaf fluttered from the tree,
"Be constant" and "be constant," still his plea.

Her simple heart with tender zeal sought long
How it might free her questioned faith from wrong :
Twofold her sorrow ; ever grieving more
That he she loved Doubt's chafing burden bore.

But, failing all the blameless arts it knew,
The simple heart from simple subtle grew :
"Thou art inconstant—*thou* ! else wouldst thou trust
The soul that leaned on thee ! "   Home went the thrust.

QUATRAINS

I

TO IMAGINATION

ONE day thou didst desert me—then I learned
How looks the world to men that lack thy grace,
And toward the shadowy night sick-hearted turned ;
When lo ! the first star brought me back thy face !

II

CONSTANCY IN CHANGE

Oh, would that thou for me a port mightst keep,
From baffling winds and tides that troubling roll ;
Thou canst not ! better then thy stormy deep
Than the calm haven of another soul !

37

III

SANS PEUR

It was because such radiant hopes were mine,

That fear did set an ambush everywhere;

It is because such hopes no longer shine,

That now a heart all proof to fear I bear.

THE DISPUTE

I

Of this plant they still dispute :
"Baneful, both the leaf and root !
He who its distillage drinks,
To Lethean darkness sinks."

"Blest the root, and blest the leaf,
Stanch restorer, cure of grief !
Quick the potion.   Baffled Death
Flees at Life's returning breath."

There the two alembics stand :
Poison dire !—elixir bland !
Of this herb they still dispute ;
Still the truth flies their pursuit.

39

II

Then was brought another plant,
Which the sages viewed askant:
" Wring from this a toxic charm ?
Nay, it hath no power for harm."

" Of its juice a cordial press?
But the weed is virtueless ! "
So each savant did reject
What he found of null effect.

Smiling scorners, this I learn :
Like the herb which ye did spurn,
That which hath no force for ill,
Neither can it good distil.

VOS NON VOBIS

I

THERE was a garden planned in Spring's young days,

Then, Summer held it in her bounteous hand;

And many wandered thro' its blooming ways;

But ne'er the one for whom the work was planned.

     And it was vainly done—

For what are many, if we lack the one?

II

There was a song that lived within the heart

Long time—and then on Music's wing it strayed!

All sing it now, all praise its artless art;

But ne'er the one for whom the song was made.

     And it was vainly done—

For what are many, if we lack the one?

SO IT WAS DECREED

Thou to lift thy good right arm,

Thou to guard her from all harm,

At the point of knightly steel,

And thy blood her triumph seal?

Nay, another claims that right,

Thrice a churl and losel knight,

Craven crest and tarnished fame,

Shield that blushes but with shame!

He whose veins shall never bleed,

He, not thou, the lance will shake,

In the lists, for her sweet sake!

Fret not.   So it was decreed.

II

Thou to soothe his weary eyes,

Kneeling where he stricken lies?

Thou the cordial to outpour,

And from swoon his breath restore?

Thou to read his lips' least sign?

Nay, another hand than thine

Yields a service cold and loath,

Listless to her wedded troth—

If his spirit stay, or speed!

She, not thou, the vigil keeps,

If he wakes, or if he sleeps.

Fret not. So it was decreed.

A SONG OF TRIBUTES

THIS is the truth of thee and me :

Many the rivers that run to the sea,

    For the river one sea—no more !

Many the flowers that lift their eyes

To the lord of the golden summer skies,

    For the flowers one sun—no more !

On, to the sea are the rivers urged,

Within the sea are the rivers merged—

    And the sea knoweth them not !

After its little span of an hour,

Blossomed and gone is the yearning flower—

    And the sun knoweth it not !

The sea that receives, or the rivers that run,

The flower, or the unbeholding sun—

 Happier, who shall say?

But this is the truth of thee and me:

Thrall of love, or loveless and free—

 Happier, who shall say?

A VISIONARY

HER love was coming from the ends of earth,

His face was toward her ; hence, between was nought ;

Seas, rocks, great woods, no bar to vision wrought,

But, sitting by her own warm, waiting hearth,

    How well she saw his face,

    And rapt, enkindled eye.

Her love was coming, day and night on night ;

To the soft stars, as he impatient came,

Oft sighingly he spake her tuneful name :

Loud roared the wintry tempest in its might,

    But she—she heard that sigh,

    And her heart beat apace.

THE POISONED RING

SLEEPS never evil that hath once had power ?

Not clods compact the venomed sting can draw !

There was a ring of old Venetia's dower,

And for its seal it bore a lion's claw.

To-day an idler, toying with that ring,

Found death was ambushed in the crafty claw ;

Not dust of time could choke the poison-spring,

Not clods compact the venomed sting could draw !

Lover of Love, forgive, if this I say—

That where poor Love hath but a single hour,

His arch-foe Hate outwears the night and day.

Sleeps never evil that hath once had power !

ULYSSES AT THE COURT OF ALCINOUS

" Pontonous gave act to all he willed,
And honey-sweetness-giving-mind's wine filled,
Disposing it in cups for all to drink."

—CHAPMAN'S *Homer*.

ONE OUTSIDE SPEAKS.

FOUNTAIN in the starlight jetting,

Fallen waters softly fretting,

Bloom of garden lost to view,

All its soul merged in the dew !

Dusk, and dew, and sweets untold

Me in nameless thraldom hold.

Past the torch-lit portal's square,

In the calmèd golden air,

Framed with purple outer shade

48

(Like a dream that cannot fade—

Like a charm Amphion-wrought,

Built by music, up from thought),

Sit Alcinous and the Court ;

While this stranger grave of port,

Clad in outland garment mean,

Swart, with eye-glance passing keen,

Lifting voice and suasive hands,

Lord of speech, in presence stands !

Here, beside the garden-pale,

Come but fragments of the tale :

'Tis of war and city's sack,

Breathless sea-toil and blind wrack.

Every word doth lodgment find

In the King's deep heart and mind ;

He who can Alcinous please

Holds of royal meed the keys :

" I was called *Shrewd Counsellor*—

You may call me *Wanderer*.

Speed me home, whose life outworn

Gropes to find its country's bourne ! ''

Ceasing now, he seems o'erwrought.

What ! the King commands be brought

That old Wine of all men's thirst,

So long since in earth immersed

None can tell what sun did shine,

In what land, upon its vine !

What ! this waif from off the sea

Taketh, as his juggler's fee,

Honey-Sweetness-Giving-Mind's Wine !

Finds all store—finds food, and finds wine,

And what else a man may covet

Here on earth, to live above it !

I have drunk of cups acerb,

Gladless wine and sullen herb,

Till my veins with bitter run ;

Yet all ill were quick undone,

Might I taste that potion blending

Calm and rapture far transcending

Sun's gold cordial, rippling wind's wine—

Honey-Sweetness-Giving-Mind's Wine !

HIMEROS

" The God of love, and benedicite !
How mighty and how great a lord is he ! "

IT shall befall,
Ere yet the wild wing'd droves
Revisit the bare groves,
That midst her wintry sleep
The World's great heart shall leap
At some far call.

At some far call,
Sets out the migrant bird ;
The drear dead grass is stirred,
The moth its prison breaks,
And each lone life partakes
The life of all.

Of old, as now,

This was that power benign—

This was that power malign

That did ordain unrest

And hunger to be blest :

To whom all bow.

To whom all bow :—

The blossom and the sod

Feel the unquiet God ;

Bird, beast, and thine own race

Strive not before his face—

Then, strivest thou ?

Despair thine art !

Thou canst not hush those cries,

Thou canst not blind those eyes,

Thou canst not chain those feet,

But they a path shall beat

Forth from thine heart.

Forth from thine heart !

There wouldst thou dungeon him,

In cell both close and dim—

The key he turns on thee,

And out he goeth free !

    Despair thine art.

    Thy bondslave—no !

But thou shalt wear his chain,

Nor meed for toil shalt gain,

But evermore be glad,

Though hungering and unclad,

    To serve him so.

    Thou'lt serve him so !

He goeth with thee, save

Into thy quiet grave ;

For he was born ere thee,

Nor ever shall he be

    With man laid low.

    Not then he tires,

When thou art smallest dust

Driven on every gust !

Still round the glowing world,

Though thou be cold, are hurled

His quenchless fires.

His quenchless fires

Brothers born after thee

(Kin of mortality)

Shall house, and welcome give ;

And lordless shall he live—

Lord of Desires !

AT SEVILLE

" There is bitter fruit at Seville—said you so ? "
" I said the fruit was sweetest there.   You know
That every sweet its bitter hath, by due ;
Who tarries there too long, shall taste the bitter too."

—Pilgrims Ever.

THERE is bitter fruit at Seville !

There the orange-groves are teeming,

And the golden spheres are gleaming

'Mid the glossy, sighing leaves,

While the fountain sings, or grieves—

As your mood is grief or revel—

To the measure of your dreaming !

     Ay !

There is bitter fruit at Seville !

There is bitter fruit at Seville !

Other singing, other sighing

56

Than the drowsy south wind dying

Off the groves at close of day—

Than the rosy fountain's play

In the sunbeam long and level—

Other singing, other sighing—

     Ay !

There is bitter fruit at Seville !

There is bitter fruit at Seville !

From the old Giralda leaning,

Many a youth and maiden, gleaning

In the orange-groves, I see.

Ambushed in the leafy tree

There's another holds his revel,

Scarce the bow and arrow screening—

     Ay!

There is bitter fruit at Seville !

There is bitter fruit at Seville !

Sweet—and bitter, for your eating !

Soon the summer will be fleeting,

Dark the Guadalquivir flows,

Chill the air from mountain snows ;

Then the winds the groves dishevel,

Through their empty aisles repeating,

"Ay !

There is bitter fruit at Seville ! "

There is bitter fruit at Seville !

Long or brief be your sojourning,

You'll not go without heartburning :

Say " adieu "—and yet " adieu ; "

But the spell is laid on you—

(Spell of angel or of devil !)

Here your soul shall be returning—

Ay de mi !

There is bitter fruit at Seville !

TIME'S WORK

" WHERE got ye that gossamer weft

For those locks that as jet were, of old ? "

    " Brushing the cobwebs of Time,

    I bore them away on my head ! "

" Where got ye those seams in the brow

And the cheek, that so smooth were, of old ? "

    " Oh, gayly fencing with Time,

    He struck me athwart with his foil ! "

" But whence is that droop of the head

(So proud as the yew-tree, of old) ? "

    " Bearing the fardels of Time,

    I stooped ever more, as I went ! "

" But the heart in the breast, that once sang

Like Memnon, in mornings of old ? "

"Half-muted the chords of that harp,

Since Time laid his hand thereupon ! "

THE TEARS OF THE POPLARS

HATH not the dark stream closed above thy head,

With envy of thy light, thou shining one?

Hast thou not, murmuring, made thy dreamless bed

Where blooms the asphodel, far from all sun?

But thou—thou dost obtain oblivious ease,

While here we rock and moan—thy funeral trees.

Have we not flung our tresses on the stream,

Hath not thy friend, the snowy cygnet, grieved,

And ofttimes watched for thy returning beam,

With archèd neck—and ofttimes been deceived?

A thousand years, and yet a thousand more,

Hast thou been mourned upon this reedy shore.

How long, how long since, all the summer day,

Earth heard the heavens sound from pole to pole,

While legion clouds stood forth in bright array ;

Yet no rain followed on the thunder's roll !

Beneath that glittering legion shrank the seas,

And fire unseen was borne upon the breeze.

The ground was smouldering fire beneath our tread,

The forest dropped the leaf, and failed all grass.

The souls of stricken men their bodies fled,

And, sighing, flocked the wind.—We heard them pass !

The priest, that scanned the portent of the skies,

Fell reeling back, with pierced and shrivelled eyes.

But ah, he saw not what our sight discerned—

The flying chariot-wheel, with fervid tire—

The steeds that unaccustomed guidance spurned

With fateful hoof and breath that scattered fire—

He saw not thee and thine unmeasured fall,

And Jove, unheeding, in his cloudy hall !

Dragged headlong by those swift immortal horse,

Up to our sire went thy vain cry for aid ;

Neither he cast a bound, to check their course,

Nor on the golden rein a hand he laid.

Brother beloved, what foe could so deceive,

Bidding thee dare what scarcely Gods achieve ?

Alas ! that we remember—and forget !

For, if we sometimes gain a brief repose,

Soon are we roused, by sudden fear beset ;

Then, through our silver boughs a shudder goes,

Our heads we lift, we search the azure gloom,

As though thou still wert falling to thy doom !

Upon the earth no loves were ever ours,

Man greets us from afar, but comes not near,

Nor even round our dark unwindowed towers

Throng the light birds—so much our grief they fear !

We sigh—we tremble—'tis not to the breeze—

Brother beloved, we are thy funeral trees !

WINTER SLEEP

I KNOW it must be winter (though I sleep)—
I know it must be winter, for I dream
I dip my bare feet in the running stream,
And flowers are many, and the grass grows deep.

I know I must be old (how age deceives !)—
I know I must be old, for, all unseen,
My heart grows young, as autumn fields grow green,
When late rains patter on the falling sheaves.

I know I must be tired (and tired souls err)—
I know I must be tired, for all my soul
To deeds of daring beats a glad, faint roll,
As storms the riven pine to music stir.

I know I must be dying (Death draws near)—

I know I must be dying, for I crave

Life—life, strong life, and think not of the grave

And turf-bound silence, in the frosty year.

SIMILITUDES OF LIFE

WHATEVER thou art I know not; but I am as these unto
    thee:
A drop of white foam, I am snatched from the wave of the
    wind-winnowed sea—
That drop to its source thou soon wilt restore.

Thou drivest me on as the dust of the earth, from a sum-
    mer-dry road,
Whirled in a column obscure; but now thou removest thy
    goad—
Lo! I am dust of the earth, as before!

Or out of the clouds, on a stream, thou sheddest a flake of
    the snow!
Whatever thou art—thou Life, I know not; I stay not to
    know
If I meet thee again, or meet thee no more!

THE PINE-TREE

I AM that magian old,

Phrygian Atys' friend, and loved of Pan.

I am any god's, to loose or hold,

But little am to man.

Thou never mayst divine me,

Either when I rave,

Chanting a hoarse stave

Back to the ruffian mob

That smite the helpless seas,

Hurtling from the cave

Of Æolus Hippotades—

Thou never canst divine me

Then, or when the winds at length resign me,

And, with a long, low sob,

I sink into a sleep

So sound and deep

That thou wouldst say with a rapt breath,

" There standeth, in a tree's shape, Death ! "

But I am not Death's, nor fear to accost

The Autumnal Frost,

Whom he sends to admonish

The sylvans all ;

At whose beck, at whose call,

Their garlands, grown sear and wannish,

Fall—fall !

If thou shouldst take from me this centred spear

Wherewith I heavenward steer,

My loss I can redeem :

From under-ranks, with fadeless green bedecked,

Slowly a new peer

I choose me, and again erect

King-shaft and steering-beam !

I am great Pan's,

Not thine, though thou mayst work me to thy plans,

Of my green honors strip me,

And bring me where the tempests clip me

Naked, and reeling in dance

Over the serried floor

Of the dark sea !

Thus do to me,

Yet vain it is for thee to seek

(Listening the singing shrouds),

What oracles I speak

Of stormy waves and tides, of stars and clouds.

I am any god's, yet, more than any other's,

I am the still-loving, star-herding Mother's.

When she is far away,

I—no facile courtier of the Day—

Behind the deep guard of my loyal boughs,

Like a true eremite,

Muse on her smile and her belov'd grave brows.

If thou be friend to Night,

And she shall rule it thus—

Thou, having joined thyself to us,

And through our dark aisles pacing free—

I will send voices down, and balms for thee !

GINEVRA OF THE AMIERI

Un giovine di nobile famiglia fiorentina di nome Antonio Rondinelli, si era invaghito di una giovinetta, parimente fiorentina, figlia di Bernardo Amieri chiamata Ginevra. Ma per quanto anche la detta giovinetta, fosse innamorata del Rondinelli, egli non potè a niun patto ottenerla dal padre, al quale piacque di darla piuttosto a Francesco Agolanti. Dopo quattro anni da questa unione, si ammalò gravemente, rimaso senza polso e non dando più alcun segno di vita, creduta morta, fu sepolta in un tumulo di sua famiglia sul cimitero del Duomo presso al Campanile. La morte però della Ginevra non fu reale ma apparente, ed una di quelle asfissiè di cui i moderni fisici hanno trovato in tante diverse malattie la esistenza—Restata la donna libera o alquanto, riavuta dal grave suo assopimento, si accorse di quel che era successo, e per sottrarsi da quel miserabile luogo, salì la piccola scala della sepoltura, illuminata da qualche raggio di luna, e dato di cozzo alla lapida, se n'uscì fuori Quindi per la più corta via, cioè per quella che rasenta la Compagnia della Misericordia, e che poi prese il nome *della Morte* da questo caso, se n'andò a casa del marito, che rispondeva nel corso degli Adimari. Ma non essendo ricevuta da lui, che dalla fioca voce e dalla bianca

71

veste la credette uno spettro, o com' egli se l'immaginò, il ritorno dell' anima della medesima ; s'incamminò alla casa de Bernardo Amieri suo padre, che abitava in Mercato Vecchio dietro S. Andrea ; e poi a quella d'uno zio li vicino, donde ebbe ripetutamente la stessa repulsa.

Abbandonatasi allora alla sua mala sorte, dicesi che si rifugiasse sotto la loggia di S. Bartolommeo nella via dei Calzaioli, dove chiedendo che morte o mercè desse fine al suo dolore, si sovvenne dell' amato suo Rondinelli, che se l'era sempre mostrato fedele. A lui dunque portatasi come il meglio potè, ne fu benignamente accolta, ristorata, e in pochi di ristabilità nella primiera salute. Fin qui l'istoria, che è passata tradizionalmente sino ai nostri giorni, non ha niente d'inverosimile. Ciocchè è malagevole a credere, è lo sposalizio della Ginevra in seconde nozze con Antonio Rondinelli, vivente ancora il primo marito, e reclamante al tribunale ecclesiastico davanti al vicario, il quale sentenziò che per essere stato disciolto il primo matrimonio dalla morte, poteva la donna legittimamente passare ad altro marito.

—*Osservatore Fiorentino, Vol. 1°, pag. 119.*

GINEVRA OF THE AMIERI

I

How fair the lily of the Tuscan field,

In gardens of the Arno-side how fair!

It blooms forever on Firenze's shield;

Her very paving-stones its image bear,

Her lamp that swings above the mouldering stair,

Her glistening wefts from many an antique loom;

The symbol in their hearts her people wear.

Pure white its leaves; within, a golden gloom,

Like sunny treasure in a sunken marble room.

II

Ay, like the treasure of a marble tomb.—

Go with me down the long, long years, secure,

And I will bring you where in silence bloom

Pure lilies gathered for a soul as pure,

Asleep for sorrow that no skill might cure.

In the dim crypt, dissolved in night, they lie,

Save as one errant moonbeam, all unsure,

Dropt like a jewel from the far-off sky,

Descends to kiss a flower-soft cheek and folded eye.

III

For sweet Ginevra, some few hours ago,

The solemn murmur in the twilight street,

The snowy cross, the pall like drifted snow,

The white-clad bearers with slow-moving feet,

The torch in double line : and now, 'tis meet

She in her fathers' lasting home be laid ;

And they who love her, for her soul entreat.

Rests none more true, as matron or as maid,

Within Maria del Fiore's holy shade.

IV

Here had she come in griefless years gone by,

Here as a child that looks on those who weep,

And, wondering, asks what thing it is to die.

 A narrow cell she saw, and still, and deep;

Then down the little ladder would she creep

 With lightsome feet; but when the chilly floor

They touched, close by her mother she would keep,

 Nor ceased to watch o'er head the glimmering door,

  But danced for joy when in the sun she stood once

   more.

V

And now she dreams she lies in marble rest

 Within the Amieri's chapel-tomb,

With hands laid idly on an idle breast.

 How sweetly can the carven lilies bloom,

 As they would soften her untimely doom . . . .

 Nay, living flowers are these that brush her cheek!

She starts awake amid the nether gloom,

 From out dead swoon returning faint and weak;

  No voice hath she, but none might hear her, could she

   speak.

VI

Vaguely she reaches from her stony bed :

   The blessed moonbeam, gliding underground,

Like angel ministrant from Heaven sped,

   To rescue one in frosty irons long bound,

Cheers her new-beating heart, till she has found

   Recourse of memory and use of will.

Then, soon her feet are on the ladder-round,

   The stone above gives way to patient skill ;

   And now the wide night greets her, bright, and lone,
     and still.

VII

She scarce can know the city of her birth,

   The magic of the full moon changeth all :

There is no stir in air, no sound on earth,

   Save where, in dim recesses of the wall,

Soft-throated muffled voices may recall

   The doves that dwell with Mary of the Flower.

Anon she trembles at her own footfall,

And while the great bell sounds the dwindled hour,

She flits across the dark that falls from Giotto's tower.

VIII

A moment—one—the moon's revealing light,

 On floating robe and falling locks were shed ;

Then in a narrow street she turned forthright

 (It still remaineth surnamed of The Dead) ;

A passage grim, the nearer way it led

 To Agolante's house. Him, loving not—

Ay, more, another loving—she had wed.

 The hand that in its dotage shaped her lot

 Nor chided she, nor once her wifely state forgot.

IX

Yet days had been (who knoweth not such days ?)

 Of the sweet days of spring, forlornly sweet,

When to be done with life's involved maze,

 And on the other side to set the feet,

Far better seemed than long days to complete,

77

That drag from dawn to dusk, from dusk to dawn.

Then might one love, unblamed, from Heaven's high seat,

In spirit near, the more from sense withdrawn.

Thus had she loved three days, had life indeed been

gone.

X

Oft musing in this wise her fingers stopped

Midway their task, deserted of the mind;

Then down upon her supple knees she dropped,

And prayed to Heaven that she might guidance find.

And sometimes, were her swimming eyes inclined

Toward gray San Miniato's reverend height,

Where wondrous marble windows, not quite blind,

Transmit betimes a little flickering light :

So much, no more, she wist, hath man of spirit sight.

XI

But ah ! had she divined her own white soul

(Now likened to that strange marmoreal pane

Which, when the sun is at the western goal,

    Smiles inwardly, and takes a rosy stain),

Then had she known that marble's self were vain

    To keep the sun of love from shining through.

Meanwhile, as spring did wane her strength did wane ;

    Ofttimes a legion world of darkness flew

    Before her sight, and then with pain her breath she

       drew.

XII

It was the third day since that heavy noon,

    When she, in blinded chamber shut away,

Lost the warm feeling of rich-hearted June,

    And ghostly tapers, with oblivious ray,

Usurped the sunshine of the living day.

    Across the ancient threshold, heeding nought,

Had she been carried, mourned as soulless clay ;

    And now, but half-restored to sense and thought,

    Before her own closed doors she stood, and entrance

       sought.

XIII

Firenze's palace walls are blocks of stone,

    That, bodied thick and huge as forest oak,

Might seem the timbers brought from groves o'erthrown

    (And petrified long since), where genii broke

And hewed the rugged trunks with thunderous stroke.

    Firenze's palace-doors are massive wood,

That might seem all of stone to one who woke

    And wandered from the dead, and, wavering, stood—

Like poor Ginevra, chilled and dazed with solitude.

XIV

She knocks, with hands late-folded in the tomb;

    Benumbed, as yet not touched to human tears.

Opens the window of an upper room—

    Charily opens, and a form appears.

And now, a well-known querulous voice she hears.

    Sweet Heaven ! what word is this that strikes to kill?

It addeth horror to her dismal fears.

Beat manly hearts in manly bosoms still,

Or timorous clods for hearts, unstirred to good or ill?

XV

This word it was that smote afresh her life:

" Thou shadow of a form and voice, away !

Thou seeming voice and image of that wife

   Of whom my soul within me oft would say,

' Thee never did she love, and never may ! '

   More like, not she, some subtle fiend thou art,

Of those that lead fond piteous men astray.

   So may I not be led, despite thine art ;

   And here, by holy rood, I bid thee hence depart ! ''

XVI

Sharply the window closes on the night.

   Cease beating at the door, cease to make moan,

Thou poor Ginevra ! pity for thy plight

   Shall sooner draw the tears from very stone

Than he who, centred on himself alone,

To pluck his soul from out the demon snare,

Shall turn to think of other than his own.

There leave him, rooted on his knees in prayer,

As best he may, this night of terrors to outwear.

XVII

Mercato Vecchio shows, by morning light,

A cheerful face and sends a joyous hum.

The stalls with wealth of tinsel wares are bright,

And the good peasants with their traffic come—

With flowers and fruits, with birds in cages, some ;

But when its throngs are sleeping far away,

And the great night has made it trebly dumb,

It is a place where none would wish to stay ;

And past its emptied court Ginevra's journey lay.

XVIII

At last, at last, her weighted footsteps near

Her father's house, and hope revives apace.

How the old garden feels the crescent year !

Upon the walls the ivies interlace,

To stay the feet of Dian's marble race.

  The myrtle and the jasmine sweets exhale

That steep in wine of Asti all the place :

  But now, the odors of the box prevail—

  Fresh, bitter fresh, like wounding memories last to fail.

XIX

There was within the garden-wall a door

  Whose spring mysterious, in her childish days,

Had challenged her discovery evermore.

  But long since had she learned its baffling ways:

And soon the moonlit fountain meets her gaze,

  With the grim lion couchant just beneath.

Still from his throat the gurgling crystal plays ;

  His ready claws the creepers hold in sheath,

  And round his manèd neck they throw an airy wreath.

XX

A living presence in the place she feels,

  That makes her glance about the shade.

The garden-seat beneath the palm reveals

    Her father's self with years and slumber weighed.

Her heart's quick-bounding impulse she has stayed—

    To clasp his neck with fond encircling arm.

So, some few steps away she stands, afraid

    Ill-timed surprise may work him mortal harm,

    Or madness, never healed by cordial or by charm.

XXI

Some steps away in moonlight space she stands;

    And in a tender, broken voice, and low,

Outreaching toward him both her hands,

    Repeats a playful name used long ago,

That he her old familiar self may know.

    The aged sleeper woke from dreams unblest—

Woke with a cry descending like a blow,

    To stab the hope new-risen in her breast,

    That happier were, composed in lasting stony rest.

XXII

" And dost thou still upbraid me, spirit now,

   As thou with looks, not words, hast ever done,

Because I bade thee break the idle vow

   In childhood changed with Rondinelli's son,

Since better elsewhere wast thou wooed and won.

   But oh, that father's love should reap such spite,

A father's care at every point undone !

   Thou wast a mute reproach, while in my sight,

   And now thou leav'st the dead, to steal my rest at

      night ! "

XXIII

While senile chatterings shake his wasted frame,

   She, spirit-like, hath vanished from the spot.

Back to himself with foolish tears he came,

   Seeing that all which vexed him so was not—

Was but a filmy dream.   " Yet dreams, God wot,

   Do truer seem than truth when we are old.

But had my daughter lived, not thus forgot

Had I been sleeping on the marble cold :

My daughter rests—poor lamb!—she rests in Jesu's
fold."

XXIV

There is a festa in the middle time

Of glowing summer—St. Zenobio's Day,

When all the streets do bloom from early prime.

A little trellis, wreathed with blossoms gay,

They hang above the window, whence, they say,

The holy man looked forth with godly cheer ;

Howe'er that be, remains the blossomed spray,

And none will pluck it down, tho', wan and sear,

It sighs so mournfully amid the wintry year !

XXV

Now with a quick and keen remembering,

Ginevra finds the symbol of her fate

In St. Zenobio's flowers that cling, and cling,

And long outlast the joyous summer's date.

Since earthly portal and celestial gate

Alike refuse a shelter to her head,

She grows uncertain of her own estate :

And what if it be so—as they have said—

She lives not now, but comes a dreamer from the dead ?

XXVI

More lightly then she moved, like blessed ghost

To earth on gentlest visitation bent ;

And by the old wool-market's doorway crossed.

Above, the sculptured lamb, most innocent,

Looks back, and bears in docile young content

Its banner of the Guelph or Ghibelline.—

On, with undeviating step she went,

As one that follows out a clear design ;

Whereto hath Heaven itself vouchsafed its seal divine.

XXVII

In Via Calzaioli stood, of old,

The house of Rondinelli.   (Stands it yet,

While Time and Chance their ruinous courses hold?

   Albeit Florence, like a gem reset,

Shines with mild splendor none can e'er forget.)

   For sad Ginevra in that house abode

One whom she loved, yet not in years had met,

   Nor e'er might meet upon her earthly road.

   Now all was changed, since she had dropped her mortal
     load.

XXVIII

Thus in her thought she wanders, wide astray,

   Brain-sick with troubles of the lingering night;

When from one window gleams a candle-ray.

   It was the first sweet, charitable light

In all that dismal round had blessed her sight.

   A form within the window she discerns,

Of one who gazes, lone as eremite,

   A moment on the silent Heaven, then turns,

   To seek a weary couch where no repose he earns.

XXIX

Unto the silent Heaven, where, he deemed,

  His only love was gone, he raised his eyes ;

And, it might be, awhile entranced he dreamed

  He saw her own unclose, in glad surprise,

To meet the rosy dawn in Paradise.

  But, even now, a voice is in his ears—

Like tenderest wind-voices—voice of sighs—

  Melodious, wandering, vague ; at last, more clear,

  It fulls, in tones at once memorial and dear.

XXX

" To thee, I come, because no more I live.

  Rejoice therefor, nor be by doubt oppressed.

'Tis Heaven, Antonio, doth my warrant give.

  Though from the dead, I walk a spirit blest,

Permitted to fulfil so high behest ;

  For henceforth, by my guiding care constrained,

Thou shalt not miss thy way to heavenly rest.

And know, if it can soothe a heart long pained,

That I did love thee well—how well !—while life re-

mained.''

XXXI

There ceased the voice, there utterly it ceased.

    She fell, as drift of snow dislodged might fall—

As silently ; as if, indeed, released,

    Her troubled spirit had surmounted all.

One moment—one—enchantment's idle thrall

    Antonio at the window stood aghast ;

Then the long staircase and the echoing hall,

    With blurrèd candle, breathlessly he passed.

    The chained and bolted door withstands, but yields at

      last.

XXXII

Beside her, down upon the stone he kneels ;

    And, uttering many a hurried, tremulous word,

Her languid wrists for sign of life he feels.

    Then suddenly to him a test occurred,

Which in familiar lore he oft had heard :

  To hold before her lips the candle flame,

To try, if ne'er so faintly, it were stirred.

  Ah, joy ! the breath of being went, and came,

  And a light tremor ran along her slender frame.

XXXIII

Then did he lift her in his two strong arms,

  And bear her up the stair, with single thought

How he might save her from all rude alarms,

  With which a throngèd waking might be fraught.

And therefore, he his precious burden brought

  The nearest way into a chapel small,

Where Heaven's mercy he ofttimes had sought,

  And where, now half in shadow, from the wall

  Del Sarto's Virgin gazed—the sweetest face of all.

XXXIV

So gazed the dear Madonna, dimly sweet,

  Upon Ginevra waking from her swoon,

And on Antonio kneeling at her feet,

    Transfigured all, beneath the saintly moon.

Her curving lips part smilingly, and soon

    Make murmur, half caressing, half a prayer;

" Be praise unto our Lady for this boon,

    That we one death, one heavenly entrance share.—

    The glory, even now, rests on thy brows and hair ! "

XXXV

But swift the change that o'er her features passed,

    Infinite trouble in her pleading eyes ;

" Tell me, for all my soul is overcast,

    How, if we two are havened in the skies,

This grief of the old earth can also rise.

    Surely, I from the grave myself set free,

And, wandering in white funereal guise,

    All fled when they my phantom shape did see ;

    Yet thou, if this be true—thou hast no fear of me ! "

XXXVI

" No fear of thee—no, not if thou, indeed,

    Were spirit all, and sight of thee could kill."

His words her blind imprisoned senses freed;

    Truth like a frost-wind rushed upon her chill:

" Alas, then, thou and I are living still,

    And still must linger in this world unkind ! "

In his strong arms he soothèd her until

    She found a voice and clear-remembering mind,

    To tell him what had chanced since her the grave re-

      signed.

XXXVII

And when her mournful story all was told

    To where he found her fallen at his door,

Her voice broke off with sobbings manifold:

    " And I have learned—oh, knowledge wounding sore !

That they who loved me once do love no more.

    Yet must I their unwilling shelter seek,

Where only bitterness can be in store.

    I know not what to do—I am too weak

    With the great load of life and death—but do thou

        speak."

XXXVIII

Spoke then the voice of love, long years uppent,

    Freed, as the rivers from their flood-gates be,

When rains of Heaven a vernal force have lent.

    " Ay, let me speak—and thou, give heed to me

Whose soul is bowed, the while I bend the knee.

    My own Ginevra—mine !   Nay, do not start ;

It has befallen by divine decree

    That thou may'st safely shelter in my heart,

    Though we but lately stood the breadth of Heaven

        apart."

XXXIX

" Ah ! better now, with all the holy dead,

    To be at rest than on such counsel lean ! "

" Nay, hear my counsel to the end," he said ;

" It is because thou with the dead hast been,

Thou dwellest not within the Law's demesne ;

    But void is every bond aforetime made.

When death or death-like trance doth supervene,

    The veriest wretch that once his doom hath paid

    May henceforth rest secure—the hand of Law is stayed.

XL

" Thou wast too young, or well thou could'st recall

    The Lady Federiga—true and fond,

And therefore hurried past a convent wall.

    Despite her vows, she sank in Love's despond.

One night her soul, like thine, did stray beyond

    This limitary life : returned again,

Our Mother Church absolved her from her bond ;

    Since, having deemed her dead, it could no more con-
        strain.

    Some months flew by, and those who loved, the Church

        made twain.''

XLI

She listens, and belief gains way the while :

  " Antonio, Truth and thou wert ever one,

Nor could'st thou change so much, to treat with guile

  A creature whose good days beneath the sun

But lately were like sands almost outrun."

  " Soul of my soul !　I have not changed, I swear !

Say only what thou would'st—it shall be done :

  And thou may'st seek, till we one home do share,

  The pitying sisterhood and St. Umiltà's care."

XLII

What sorcery in the moon's all-blanching beam,

  To steal the rose of life from those we know,

When, like the haunting sculpture of a dream,

  Pallid and strange those household faces show.

But on Ginevra's cheek a living glow

  Came with the kiss upon her forehead laid ;

She looked as she did look full long ago,

When each to other felt their being swayed

In Love's mysterious dawn, that held them half-afraid.

XLIII

There was a chamber opening toward the West,

    Where burned, all times, a pale and starry light.

The sportive name of Filomela's Nest

    It once had borne; but, lost to mortal sight,

The singing-bird had winged a silent flight.

    " Thou in my sister's room a guest shall be,

Where, since she slept, none e'er hath passed a night.

    Of all who gave her love, she most loved thee:

    Her spirit there shall breathe, and thou shalt trust in

      me.''

XLIV

So saying, once again he lifted her,

    And soon, amidst the pillows' driven snow,

She slept as though all sorrows cancelled were,

    That have been or can be on earth below.

His eyes her sleeping face could not forego;

And Love kept guard, as of a miser's thrift;

For, the once-wandered spirit—who can know?—

    May find again the still unknitted rift,

    And slip away; and thus, the Gods recall their gift.

XLV

Adieu, thou tenderest wanderer, adieu!

    'Tis strange to leave thee ere thy joy-bells ring,

For I have traced each way thy footsteps knew,

    And followed all thy drear night-journeying;

And seen thy Blossom-City crowned with spring,

    The while, thy story's fragrant crypt unsealed,

The winds of Time such sweetness brought—and bring!

    How fair the lily of the Tuscan field,

    And still, how fair it blooms upon Firenze's shield!

SONNETS

MOTHER ENGLAND

I

THERE was a rover from a western shore,

England! whose eyes the sudden tears did drown,

Beholding the white cliff and sunny down

Of thy good realm, beyond the sea's uproar.

I, for a moment, dreamed that, long before,

I had beheld them thus, when, with the frown

Of sovereignty, the victor's palm and crown

Thou from the tilting-field of nations bore.

Thy prowess and thy glory dazzled first;

But when in fields I saw the tender flame

Of primroses, and full-fleeced lambs at play,

Meseemed I at thy breast, like these, was nursed;

Then mother—Mother England! home I came,

Like one who hath been all too long away!

II

As nestling at thy feet in peace I lay,
A thought awoke and restless stirred in me :
" My land and congeners are beyond the sea,
Theirs is the morning and the evening day.
Wilt thou give ear while this of them I say :
' Haughty art thou, and they are bold and free,
As well befits who have descent from thee,
And who have trodden brave the forlorn way.

Children of thine, but grown to strong estate ;
Nor scorn from thee would they be slow to pay,
Nor check from thee submissly would they bear ;
Yet, Mother England ! yet their hearts are great,
And if for thee should dawn some darkest day,
At cry of thine, how proudly would they dare ! ' "

THE TRAITORS' GATE

At the Tower of London

Thou low-browed, fateful archway to the Thames!

I stood beside the long-shut gate, and thought

Of all those sad ones who were hither brought

In barge as mournful as the barque that stems

The stream of fabled shades, where no star gems

The utter night, and sighs and prayers are naught.

Here 'twas to part with all aforetime sought—

Love, pleasures, civic honors, diadems.

The Traitors' Gate? How Time that word belies!

Who now but hath at heart a spring of tears

For him, great voyager of other years—

Fain to meet death beneath the open skies;

Or her, who, closing not, her lovely eyes,

Filled the rude headsman's soul with nameless fears!

OLD-WORLD BELLS

How merrily they ring—these old-world bells,

These old-world bells—how pitiless they ring!

Whether at daybreak an aubade they fling,

Or with increase of night the burden swells,

Forever and forevermore it tells

(Or dark or light the time) one only thing—

How swift the hour, the year, the ages spring,

Mindless of human greetings and farewells.

Ye tongues exultant!   Wherefore all for mirth,

Hastening the hour that hastes to come and go?

For never do ye sound one note of woe,

Though ye were formed and raised by hands of earth.

Forgetful of your fashioners ye grow,

Allegiant to the skies, and lost to all below.

OPEN WINDOWS

THANK God, the cold is gone, the summer here !

My spirit, long shut in, once more is free,

And feels its kindred in yon bounteous tree,

Where all day long birds sing their loves' sweet cheer.

No longer, with bare thorns and few leaves sere,

· Taps on the pane, in dreary monody,

The eglantine ; but now she lures the bee,

Her face bedewed with many a morning tear.

No longer toil the streams in crystal bounds ;

Nor veil of snow dims now the plains or heights ;

Nor mask of glass between us and the sky :

Through open windows float all gladdening sounds,

Through open windows come all cheerful sights—

My soul through open windows breathes a grateful sigh !

105

THE WIND OF SPRING

AMONG the chill and early days of spring,

Comes sometimes one all glittering gold and gray ;

A swift heraldic wind goes on its way,

And no place is but feels its visiting.

"Wake ! wake !" and ever "wake," I hear it sing.

And now, all things respond as best they may ;

The branches toss, the forest pillars sway,

The old leaves of the year take rustling wing.

But soon into the joyous tumult creeps

A faint, a shuddering voice (I only know

'Tis not the sighing of the withered grass,

Nor clash of boughs where yet the leaf-bud sleeps) :

"We would awake—we cannot wake !" Alas,

I heard it not in springs of long ago.

SUNSET

WHAT pageants have I seen, what plenitude

Of pomp, what hosts in Tyrian rich array,

Crowding the mystic outgate of the day;

What silent hosts, pursuing or pursued,

And all their track with wealthy wreckage strewed.

What seas that roll in waves of gold and gray,

What flowers, what flame, what gems in blent display—

What wide-spread pinions of the phœnix brood ?

Give me a window opening on the west

And the full splendor of the setting sun.

There let me stand and gaze, and think no more

If I be poor, or old, or all unblest;

And when my sands of life are quite outrun,

May my soul follow thro' the day's wide door!

AND DESIRE SHALL FAIL

RESOLVE me why, in undiverted quest,

We spend our most of life beneath the sun,

Unquenched the prime desire, the goal but one,

Ev'n as the morning's flight is toward the west—

Resolve me why, soon as our feet have pressed

The wished-for bound (the long race being run),

Desire itself sinks down outworn, undone,

Till of possession we are dispossessed !

A starveling who, once seated at the feast,

That moment craves no more to eat or drink—

A traveller, who, beside the fountain's brink,

Finds suddenly his thirst unslaked hath ceased—

A dungeon prisoner, who, to light released,

Smiles vacantly upon the broken link !

THE SHADOW

LEAVE me in peace but for a little space,

Old Shadow ever hovering near, more near !

Ev'n from a child, how many and how dear

Have I beheld depart with changed, strange face,

Until thou art in every time and place :

Thine is the waning and the budding year,

The undernote in every song I hear !

Leave me in peace to end my little race.

If there be any light to blot thee out,

Or kindly darkness deeper than thou art,

May I thine image sometimes soothly miss !

They whom I loved—my love they will not doubt,

Nor grieve (if they in any world have part)

That I should find some remnant joy in this.

DOUBT

THERE may be canker at the rose's core,

An arrow through the summer darkness flying—

A poisoned breath in the green leaves' low sighing,

And bane from Trebizond our bees may store ;

And thou, whose face makes sunshine at my door—

How know I but those sweetest lips be lying,

And in their perjuries thine eyes complying,

What time they say, "Trust us forevermore?"

But no ! beneath what seems I'll not be prying,

Not though the rose have canker at its core—

My love, not though thy sweetest lips be lying !

To doubt, were to receive some wounding score

Each hour—each day and morrow to be dying ;

To Death I yield, but not to Doubt, who slays before !

A FEW GREAT THINGS

A FEW great things our mortal essence bound,

And in its primal health man's being keep ;

Such are light, breath, and food and drink, and sleep:

As though not lapped in mystery profound,

With these the thankful Life fulfils her round.

Happy, whose senses glow, whose pulses leap—

The gypsy on the heath's wide, windy sweep—

The youth absorbed in dreams—the victor crowned !

A few great things the soul of man sustain ;

These are its breath of life, its food, its rest:

Some few to love us (one to love us best),

And faith in God no trouble can distrain ;

Or proud, or lowly, they who entertain

These goodly things, shall be of all possessed.

HOMESICKNESS AT SEA

WITH the sweet Earth my sole allegiance lies,

In her firm arms I only am at rest.

I am her child ; and, leaning on her breast,

Hear her great heart-throbs and her tender sighs ;

Nor save through her know I the bending skies.

Alien, I drive before the billowy crest ;

By the void baseless deep I am oppressed,

And desolate 'mid its inhuman cries.

Such homesickness besets me on the sea,

When I my Mother Earth have left behind,

So one in one with her, my loves are twined :

Such homesickness within my soul shall be,

When I before the winds of time must flee,

And no well-known, green, sunlit shore shall find.

ANTÆUS

THE gods are on the lawless giant's track,

With fulmined bolts and arrows they pursue ;

Yet, though they pierce his great heart thro' and thro',

And though they stretch him on the torture-rack

Till all his mighty thews and sinews crack,

See what the ancient healing Earth can do—

How quick his ebbèd powers she will renew,

As to her vital bosom he sinks back !

Take lesson from the Titan, O thou sage :

Pain and confusion wait on him who pries

Into the secret of the jealous skies.

Yet, if thou wilt on airy quest engage,

Bethink thee often of thine heritage—

Touch the sane Earth, where all thy safety lies !

INTERPRETATION OF NATURE

YONDER the self-same star, with self-same glance,

Is looking on a hundred lands to-night,

On vale, and nestling town, and mountain height,

Wherever man hath his inhabitance.

The lover, gazing in delicious trance,

Hath his own reading of that rubric bright ;

Another fills the dim and fading sight

Of him who looks his last on Heaven's expanse.

There is one murmur of the tided deep,

But many are the voices set thereto ;

And, at the wind's wild clarion, souls upleap,

Or shrink as fleeing deer when hounds pursue.

O Nature, lend thyself to smile—to weep—

To do whate'er we human creatures do !

HEREAFTER

HEREAFTER shalt thou hear (who hast not heard),

Hereafter shalt thou see (who hast not seen),

Hereafter, when void Silence falls between !

Then shall come back her futile heart-wrung word ;

Then, the film'd glances of the wounded bird,

The fluttering hand, the whole slow drooping mien.

Hereafter, shall thine eye and ear be keen,

And from the very depths thou shalt be stirred.

—I err : for never shalt thou hear, or see ;

Nor Memory, nor great Death, shall teach thee aught

Of her, thine own—whom little thou dost know ;

Recognizance nor grief shall come to thee,

But on my soul such record shall be wrought,

That I shall see and hear her—I, who love her so !

THE BOOK OF DEEDS AND DAYS

WIDE open lay the Book of Deeds and Days,

Whose secret none of all that live may win.

—And now, at last, I was to read therein.

I met my Angel's subtle-smiling gaze:

" Look ! read !   And faint not in thy first amaze ! "

Trembling, and loth such venture to begin,

I found a passage that, methought had been

Illustrate with good deeds and starred with praise;

Thereunder was inscribed one word—*Alas !*

A heavenly zephyr quickly turned that leaf;

How shone my obscure day with trial fraught !

I read, *By this into the Kingdom pass.*

Then said that Angel, void of joy or grief,

" Stands no man's compt as he himself had thought."

THE GREAT CIRCLE

WHOEVER journeys from his native earth,

From sea to sea, from sky to sky, so far,

The vault holds not for him one well-known star ;

His footsteps having traced the world's wide girth,

At last he sees the smoke from his own hearth,

And sits again before the genial Lar,

And dreams, perchance, he never crossed the bar,

Nor left at all the loved land of his birth.

If now, an errant path my wanderings show,

'Tis only the Great Circle I complete,

That hath its source and end in Love !—I go

But to return unto my spirit's seat—

A blest home-comer, by the ingle-glow,

Forgetting alien triumph or defeat !

THE CHILD-SELF

TO S. F. G.

AH, how we change and change, as years slip by !

Surely, our former selves no more remain ;

Such strangers to the pleasure, to the pain,

That made our hearts go slow, or bounding high.

Yet sometimes that looks forth within the eye,

Which brings the long past sweetly home again,

Ev'n as the ancient Presence in a fane

Might answer to the latest pilgrim's sigh.

Children were we together—mark it well.

Man, as he journeys on, drops youth, drops prime,

Drops all—like a cast garment threadbare worn.

Drops all ?—ah, no ; for from old Age's cell

Thro' tumults of midday, from time to time,

The Child-Self sends that startled look of morn !

A PRAYER FOR SUBTLETY

WEAK as I am, I have not prayed for power
As they who, right or wrong, would fain be felt;
But unto Heaven daily have I knelt,
That gentlest subtlety be in my dower,
Such as, of old, made false Duessa cower,
Such as, of old, obdurate stone could melt,
And set those spirits free, who long had dwelt,
Devoid of hope, in some enchanter's tower.

So might I draw the stray lamb from its foe,
The traveller lure away from ambushed harm;
But most of all (since woman's heart I bear)
When from the Sirens' reef sweet voices flow,
Might I, with sweeter tones, in counter-charm,
Save great Ulysses from the watery snare!

DISCOVERY

What is there left our spirits to discover ?

No continent beyond the sea lies veiled ;

The plunging diver, in strange armor mailed,

Has searched its floor while cumbering tides swept over !

Before us, up the clouds has gone a rover—

Victorious where Dædalian boldness failed !

The very stones—the flowers, by name are hailed,

Though round their sweets the simple bees yet hover.

What more remains?   Enamoured of the rod,

Pale saints and seers Divinity have shown.

Enough ! why seek we a new name for God !

What then remains ?—For us, for each alone,

Here to tread out the way, before untrod,

Of each sole life—and forth into the Wide Unknown.